Judy Moody & Stink

THE HOLLY JOLIDAY

Books About Judy:

 Books About Stink:

 Books About Judy and Stink:

Judy Moody & Stink

THE HOLLY JOLIDAY

Megan McDonald

illustrated by Peter H. Reynolds

CANDLEWICK PRESS

Text copyright © 2007 by Megan McDonald
Illustrations copyright © 2007 by Peter H. Reynolds
Judy Moody font copyright © 2003 by Peter H. Reynolds

Judy Moody®. Judy Moody is a registered trademark of Candlewick Press, Inc.

"You're a Mean One, Mr. Grinch"
Lyrics by Dr. Seuss, Music by Albert Hague
© 1966 (Renewed) Ted Geisel Publishing and Albert Hague
All Rights Controlled by EMI Robbins Catalog Inc. (Publishing)
and Alfred Publishing Co., Inc. (Print)
All Rights Reserved   Used by Permission

First paperback edition 2008

Library of Congress Cataloging-in-Publication Data is available.

Library of Congress Catalog Card Number 2007933577

ISBN 978-0-7636-3237-3 (hardcover)
ISBN 978-0-7636-4113-9 (paperback)

12 13 14 15 16 17 TWPS 11 10 9 8 7 6

Printed in Singapore

This book was typeset in Stone Informal and Judy Moody.
The illustrations were done digitally.

Candlewick Press
99 Dover Street
Somerville, Massachusetts 02144

visit us at www.candlewick.com

For my family
M.M.

To the family who knows how to celebrate
year-round—the Doucettes of Dedham, Mass....
Bill, Cheryl, Alex, and Ian!
P.H.R.

CONTENTS

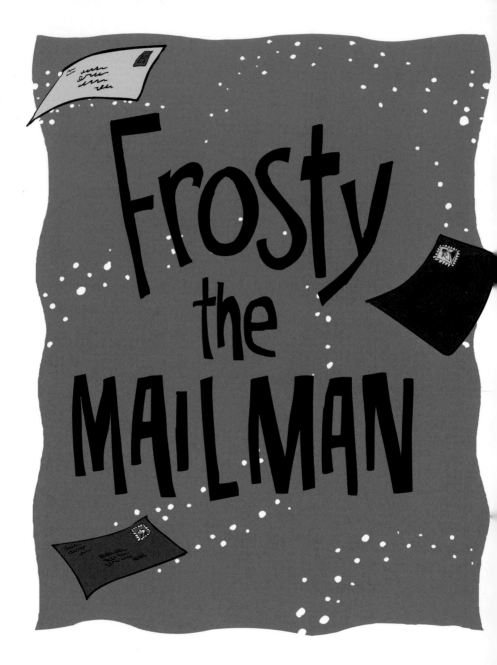

Stink was glued to the weather channel, when out on the porch he heard such a clatter! *Thunk! Clunk!* Stink sprang from the sofa to see what was the matter. "Mailman!" he shouted with glee. "Somebody got a package!"

"Stink, I hope you didn't write more letters and order more free stuff," Judy called after him. "Mom and Dad will be mad."

"Nope," said Stink, opening the door and running down the walk to catch the mail truck before it pulled away. He liked talking to Mr. Harvey, the mailman. Mr. Harvey had a ponytail and a dog named Pork Chop.

"How's Pork Chop?" Stink asked, but when the mailman turned around, it wasn't the mailman at all. He did not have a ponytail. And he did not look like someone who had a dog named Pork Chop.

This guy had white fuzzy hair and smiley wrinkles. He had a white bushy beard and hairy eyebrows, and he wore a furry hat with the earflaps turned up. He did not look like a mailman.

"Who are you?" asked Stink. "And where's Mr. Harvey?"

"I'm the new guy," said the not-

mailman. "Glad to meet you. My name's Frost. Call me Jack," said Mr. Frost, grinning and winking and raising his bushy white eyebrows.

"No way! You mean *you're* Jack Frost? For real? Like the snowman? Like the guy that paints frosty pictures on leaves and windows?"

"That's me," said the mailman. "And guess what happens when a dog bites me?"

"What?" Stink asked.

"I get *Frost* bite," Jack said, grinning. Stink howled over that one.

Jack Frost handed Stink two more boxes. "Special delivery today. These didn't fit in your mailbox."

4

"Are any from the North Pole?" Stink shook the boxes. One was from the L. L. Beanery and smelled like coffee. The other one was as heavy as books but sounded like . . . fruitcake! Sick!

"Probably just fruitcake," said Stink. "My grandma Lou sends us one every year around the holidays. Our cat, Mouse, is the only one who eats it!"

"Better luck next time, huh?" Jack said.

"Hey, if you're Jack Frost," said Stink, "I was wondering . . . do you think you could deliver snow this year? All I want for Christmas is snow."

"Snow, huh? Well, you never know. Might be able to arrange it for you this year."

"You can do that?" Stink asked. "For real?"

Jack Frost laughed and tugged at his white beard, winking and looking up at the sky. "From what I can tell, there's a low-pressure system moving in. Cold front could get here as early as this weekend."

"Wow!" said Stink. "So you can predict the weather, too?"

"I've been in this line of work for a lot of years. I can feel the weather in my bones." Jack Frost stuck out his tongue. "Right now, I can almost taste snow in the air."

"I have a super-good sniffer," said Stink. "Maybe I can smell it in the air." He closed his eyes and stuck his nose in the air. *Sniff,*

sniff. He pictured catching snowflakes on his tongue. *Sniff, sniff.* He pictured a snow-ball fight. *Sniff, sniff.* He pictured a great big whopping whiteout. "Yep, I think I smell snow," said Stink.

Stink and Jack Frost were quiet for a minute. Together they looked up at the gloomy gray sky and sniffed the moist, damp air.

"My big sister says it never snows in Virginia," said Stink. "My big sister says there's too much globe warming. My big sister says there's like a billion-to-one chance for snow this year."

"Your big sister sounds pretty smart, huh?"

"She thinks so," said Stink.

"It could happen," said Jack Frost. "One winter, back in 1980, we got thirteen and a half inches in one day. Broke all the records."

"Whoa!" said Stink.

"See? You just might get your fluffy stuff after all," said Jack Frost. "Think *snow*. Feel it in your bones."

"Thanks!" said Stink. "It's lucky I ran into you—you know, to put in my order and everything."

"Well, I'm not making any promises," Jack Frost said with a wink, "but I'll sure keep my fingers crossed!"

"Cool yule!" said Stink.

. ● .

Stink came back inside singing, *"Frosty the mailman was a jolly, happy soul . . .* Wow! You're never gonna believe . . . Guess who I just met!"

"Mr. Harvey, the mailman?" said Judy, looking up from her list.

"Nope. Who's got a beard that's long and white?"

"Must be Santa."

"Wrong again. Jack Frost. I just talked to Jack Frost! No lie!"

"Really? Was the Sandman out there, too? How about the Tooth Fairy?" Judy laughed herself silly.

"Hardee-har-har. That's his real name," said Stink. "Ask him."

"Our mailman's name is Mr. Harvey," said Judy.

"Not anymore. There was a new guy out there. Mr. Frost. As in Jack. As in Jack Frost. He knows all about snow and everything. And he says I might get snow for Christmas."

"Stink, I hate to break it to you, but Jack Frost is invisible. Or as tiny as an elf or something."

"Or something," said Stink.

"First of all," said Judy, counting off on her fingers, "you can't just see him. Jack Frost sneaks around at night or way early in the morning to make frost on windows and maple leaves."

"That's what I used to think!" said Stink.

"Second, Jack Frost is NOT a mailman. I mean, what are the chances?"

"Lots of people have more than one job," Stink said.

"Third, even if he is a mailman, he wouldn't be in Virginia. He would be in Alaska or Minnesota—"

"I know! What are the chances that Mr. Harvey would just disappear and Jack Frost would show up, right here on Croaker Road, this time of year? But did you ever think maybe that's why he's here—'cause it's *our* turn to have snow? I'm telling you—he can smell it coming. His bones told him, too."

"So this Jack Frost character also has talking bones?"

"Yeah, and he said it would be no pressure to bring snow. Or low pressure. I forget."

"Stink, believe me, it hasn't snowed here for like a million years."

"Not true!" said Stink. "Jack Frost said that one winter it snowed thirteen and a half inches here in one day!"

"When was this?" asked Judy.

"Back in 1980."

"Okay, so *half* a million years. Stink, I'm telling you—"

"You're not the weatherman," Stink told Judy.

"Neither is Jack Frost. He's the *mailman*, Stink." Judy let out a little puff of air. "Wait—now you have me believing this stuff."

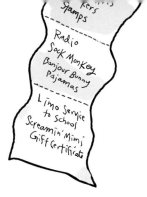

Kers
Stamps
Radio
Sock Monkey
Bonjour Bunny
Pajamas
Limo Service
to School
Screamin' Mims
Gift Certificate

Judy Moody went back to making a list and checking it twice. Not a think-up-nicknames-for-Stink list. Not a things-to-do-when-you're-home-sick list.

A T.P. (not Toad Pee) list. A toilet-paper list of all the stuff she wanted to get for Christmas. A *Totally Presents* list.

It wasn't easy writing on toilet paper. But T.P. was the only thing long enough to fit all the presents she wanted.

Judy unrolled her T.P. list. It went out the door and into the hall and past Stink's

Books
Blank Books
Art Supplies
Stickers
Stamps

Screamin' Mims
Gift Certificate
Limo Service
to School
27

room and down the stairs. It rolled right across the *S* encyclopedia Stink was reading for the one hundredth time.

"Hey!" yelled Stink.

"Sorry," said Judy. "Just making my list."

"This is like ten miles long!" said Stink.

"So? That means I get ten miles of presents," said Judy.

Stink went back to his encyclopedia. He was reading about snowy owls and snowshoe hares. He was reading about snowdrop trees. He was reading about Snowflake Bentley.

Judy didn't get it. Usually Stink wanted tons and tons of stuff. Piles more stuff than Judy. *Miles* more stuff than Judy.

"Stink, you better make a list," Judy told him. "Only five more days till Christmas."

"I already have a list," said Stink.

"Where is it?" Judy asked.

"In my head."

"You better write it down, Stinkerbell."

"I'll remember."

"How are you going to remember? If you don't write it down, how will I know what to get you? How will Mom and Dad know? And Grandma Lou? And Webster and Sophie of the Elves and any real elves?"

"Fine. I'll write it down." Stink tore a blank page from his tablet. He scribbled something in two seconds, then put his pencil down.

"Done!" said Stink.

"Done?" asked Judy. "How can you be done already? I've been working on my list for three hundred sixty-something days!"

Judy picked up the piece of paper. Stink had printed just one puny word. That one word was *snow.*

"That's it? Just one thing? Snow? That's not even a present."

"That's all I want."

"Not even snow boots or a snow hat or snow pants or snowshoes or a snow-board?"

"Nope."

"Not even an inflatable igloo with fake snowballs?"

"Nope."

"Not even a snow-globe kit or a snow-cone machine?"

"Actually, a snow-cone machine would be nice. But no. All I really want is snow."

"Stink, that is so way boring!"

"Boring? Are you cuckoo? What about snowmen and snow forts and snow angels and snowball fights? What about sledding? And what about snow days off from school?"

"Have you looked outside lately? Hel-lo! The mailman was wearing shorts the other day. And I saw a robin yesterday."

"What a grinch," said Stink.

"Stink, I told you it hardly ever even snows in Virginia. What are the chances it'll snow *this* year? For real?"

"It better snow," said Stink, "or I'm moving to Vermont."

Last day of school before Christmas!" Judy shouted when she got home from school. Judy and Stink dumped their backpacks on the couch.

"So, what did you do for your last day?" asked Mom.

"Ate candy canes," said Stink.

"We had an *Aloha* Christmas party," said Judy. "Like in Hawaii."

"Sophie of the Elves was my Secret Santa," said Stink.

"We drank pink flamingo punch and

played Pin the Monkey on the Palm Tree."

"And I got a snow globe all the way from Vermont!" said Stink.

"Mr. Todd wore sunglasses and a Hawaiian shirt and gave everybody a *lei* to wear tonight," said Judy, pointing to her flower necklace. "Don't forget that tonight is the Tenth Annual Holly Jolly Holiday Happening at school."

"We made a field guide to snowflakes," said Stink, digging into his backpack and pulling out a chart with shapes. "Even though no two are the same, a lot of snowflakes have the same shapes. Stellar dendrites are like trees, but lots of other snowflakes have shapes like pencils, prisms, plates, and puffballs."

"We learned that *Mele Kalikimaka* means Merry Christmas in Hawaii."

"We heard this story about a famous guy who figured out how to take pictures of thousands of snowflakes."

"Was his name Jack Frost?" asked Judy.

"Snowflake Bentley," said Stink. "He's in the encyclopedia. Two times. Under *S* and under *B*, too."

"In Hawaii, my name would be I-U-K-I."

"I Yucky!" said Stink. "That's the perfect name for you."

"Ho, ho, ho, Stink. You say it *Ee-oo-kee*. Your name's K-I-M-O, pronounced *Kee-mo*. I asked Mr. Todd."

"Sounds like Kimo and Iuki both had an

exciting day," said Mom. "Are you both ready for the holiday program tonight?"

"YES!" said Judy. "My class is singing 'The Twelve Days of Christmas in Hawaii'! Rare!"

"How about you, Stink? Did your class practice the skit for 'The Night Before Christmas'?"

"Don't remind me," said Stink. "I have to be a mouse again. Sophie of the Elves gets to be a sugarplum. Webster gets to be Prancer or Vixen—I forget which. But no, I have to be a shorty-pants mouse. Every year!"

"You could wear *long* pants," Judy suggested.

"At least you have a mouse costume already," said Mom.

"Yeah, put it on and give us a sneak peek. I mean a *squeak* peek." Judy cracked herself up.

"Hardee-har-har. I wish just once I could be something like . . . a stellar dendrite," Stink said wistfully.

"Stellar dandruff! Stink, there's no stellar dandruff in 'The Night Before Christmas,'" Judy teased.

Stink went upstairs to try on his mouse costume.

"And a par-rot in a palm tree." Judy practiced singing while she fed Jaws. *"And a par-rot in a palm tree."* Judy practiced singing while she put a jingle-bell collar on

Mouse. *"And a par-rot in a palm tree."* Judy practiced singing while she set the table.

Where was Stink? Why was it taking him about a hundred million years just to put on mouse ears?

Finally, Stink came downstairs, covering his not-mouse ears. "I thought there were *twelve* days of Christmas. What happened to the other eleven?"

"Ho, ho, ho," said Judy. She looked at what Stink was wearing. "Hey, where's your mouse costume? How come you're wearing all white? I thought mice were brown."

"A mouse can be white," said Stink.

"Yeah, maybe a science mouse. Like the kind that gets tests done on him. Or runs

through mazes. Or gets eaten by snakes. Not a Night-Before-Christmas mouse."

"A white mouse goes with a white Christmas," said Stink.

"Not a creature was stirring, not even a science mouse!" Judy roared.

When the Moodys got to the multipurpose room at Virginia Dare School that night, it was decorated with evergreen branches, pinecone wreaths, and candy canes. Blinking white lights twinkled around the doorway.

"The school looks so pretty tonight," said Mom.

"They did a great job," Dad agreed.

"It would look better with snow," said Stink.

"Wait till you see the decorations for our

skit," Judy told her parents. "The whole stage is going to be decked out like Hawaii. And Frank's bringing in Cookie, his real-live parrot. Cookie talks and everything!"

"Better go find your classes, you two," said Mom.

"Break a leg," said Dad.

"Look for me!" said Stink. "At the beginning of 'The Night Before Christmas.'"

"Stink, I mean Kimo, it's going to be pretty hard to miss a science mouse in the middle of a holiday celebration," said Judy.

• ● ·

The lights went down, and the Tenth Annual Holly Jolly Holiday Happening began. Ms. Tuxedo, the principal, welcomed everyone, and the music teacher played "Let It Snow" softly in the background.

Mr. Todd was the announcer, and first up was the kindergarten class, which sang the Kwanzaa Spelling Song. The fifth grade played a jazzy version of "Feliz Navidad." The first grade recited a Hanukkah poem about eight little candles. The fourth grade acted out a skit about *Sinter Klaas* from Holland. Finally, it was time for Judy's class. Judy, Rocky, and Frank stood stage left, beside Class 3T's blow-up plastic palm tree. A rainbow of pink, green, and blue spotlights shone down on them. They were all wearing shorts, flip-flops, and Hawaiian shirts.

Judy squinted in the bright light. She felt her hands sweat. She felt her neck itch under the plastic flower *lei*.

"Can you hold Cookie?" Frank asked Judy, holding out his real-live parrot. "I'm too nervous."

"I'm too nervous, too," said Judy.

"The parrot has to sit up in the palm tree," said Rocky. "Like in the song. Hurry up! Mr. Todd's about to start!"

Frank held out his arm. Cookie flapped her wings, hopping from Frank's arm onto the palm-tree prop.

"Tonight," Mr. Todd announced, "we celebrate holiday traditions from all around the world. Class 3T chose to honor

Christmas in Hawaii with its very own version of a well-known song."

Judy took a deep breath. Everyone sang:

"Number One Day of Christmas,
My tutu *gave to me*
A par-rot in a palm tree!"

Judy smiled and pushed the hair out of her eyes.

"Number Two Day of Christmas,
My tutu *gave to me*
Two pink flamingoes
And a par-rot in a palm tree!"

"Mary had a lit-tle lamb!" sang Cookie. The audience cracked up.

"Quiet, Cookie," Frank warned, shaking his finger at her.

"Number Three Day of Christmas,
My tutu *gave to me*
Three boogie boards,
Two pink flamingoes,
And a par-rot in a palm tree!"

"Mary had a lit-tle lamb!" sang Cookie, bobbing her head. The audience laughed even harder. For eleven whole verses, as soon as Class 3T sang *"parrot in a palm tree,"* Cookie squawked, *"Mary had a little lamb."*

"Twelve ukuleles,
Eleven ice cubes melting,

Ten fish a-leaping,
Nine hula dancers,
Eight Santas surfing,
Seven sharks a-swimming,
Six flip-flops flapping,
Five gol-den pineapples!
Four flower leis,
Three boogie boards,
Two pink flamingoes . . .
And a par-rot in a palm tree!"

Class 3T sang its heart out on the last verse. Just as the audience prepared to clap, Cookie sang out, *"Maria tenía un pequeño cordero!"*—"Mary had a little lamb" in Spanish! The audience went wild. They roared. They stood up and clapped. They yelled *encore*!

"Mele Kalikimaka!" shouted Class 3T, and they all took a bow before the curtains closed.

"Cookie! Bad girl!" said Frank behind the curtain. "Get down here. Right now!" He held out his arm.

"Lit-tle lamb!" sang Cookie, ruffling her feathers. But she would not come down out of the palm tree.

"All that practicing and she ruined the show!" said Frank.

"No way!" said Judy. "Everybody loved it. Cookie was the star of the show."

"They think we planned it that way!" said Rocky.

"How does Cookie know 'Mary Had a Little Lamb,' anyway?" asked Judy.

"She listens to Dog Cat Radio on the Internet," said Frank. "My mom leaves it on to keep our pets company when we're not home, and they play animal songs all day. They have a Spanish hour, too."

Mr. Todd stepped into the spotlight once more. "Thank you, Cookie the parrot, for celebrating diversity with us tonight!" Cookie bobbed her head up and down, like she was taking a bow.

"And now, for our grand finale, the second-graders will perform 'The Night Before Christmas.' "

"That's Stink's class," said Judy to Rocky and Frank. "Let's go sit in the audience so we can watch. Mrs. Dempster is reading the poem, and the kids are acting it out. Stink's the mouse. And his part's right near the beginning."

The lights went down. The audience got quiet. The curtain opened.

"'*Twas the night before Christmas,*" read Mrs. D. in a hushed voice. She was sitting in a big armchair at the front of the stage. A second-grader walked onstage, holding up a cardboard moon attached to a stick.

"*When all through the house . . .*" Mrs. D.

continued. Three more second-graders dragged a cardboard house onstage.

"Not a creature was stirring . . ." read Mrs. D. *"Not even a mouse."*

The whole audience got super still. Not a cell phone was sounding, not even a cough.

"Where's Stink?" Judy whispered. "That's his line."

"Not even a *mouse*," Mrs. D. read again, a little louder.

"Oh, no!" Judy whispered. "Stink missed his cue!"

The audience fidgeted. Chairs squeaked. Feet shuffled.

"MOUSE!" Mrs. D. said again, practically shouting this time.

 46

"Where is he?" asked Judy. Before Mrs. D. could say *mouse* again, someone—or something—burst onstage in a flash of white.

Frank Pearl leaned forward, trying to see. "Is that Stink?"

"I thought you said he was a mouse," Rocky whispered.

"He is," said Judy. "A bright, white *science* mouse!"

But when the spotlight found Stink, he was not a science mouse. He was not a mouse at all.

He was a snowflake! A bright, shiny snowflake. Stink was dressed all in white, and strapped to his back was a giant, six-pointed sparkly snowflake. On his T-shirt, in black letters, he'd written STELLAR DENDRITE.

"I can't look," said Judy, covering her face.

"Not a creature was stirring!" yelled Stink, whirling and twirling in the spotlight. "Not even a snowflake!"

It was clear from the look on her face that Mrs. Dempster had not expected a blizzard. But after Stink floated around for a moment or two, she kept right on reading the poem, as if nothing strange had happened.

Judy had known Stink to be a mouse plenty of times. She had known him to be a human flag. She had known him to be James Madison, Shortest President Ever. But never in a million years had she dreamed that Stink would one day dance onstage as a stellar dendrite.

"What a flake," said Judy. "As in *snow*flake. Or should I say, snow *freak*?" Judy and Stink would be laughing like a bowl full of jelly over this one for many Christmases to come.

It *was* the night before Christmas, and all through the house, the Moodys were stirring, even Mouse. Dad was ordering Hawaiian pizza (with pineapple!), and Mom was wrapping presents. Stink was shaking presents as fast as Mom could wrap them, then tucking them under the tree in the front room. Mouse chased a jingle bell all over the house.

She, Judy Moody, sang,

"Mele Kalikimaka *is the thing to say*
On a bright Hawaiian Christmas day!"

and

*"Have a hula, jula Christmas!
It's the best time of the year . . ."*

Dad poked his head into the playroom off the kitchen. "Pizza will be here any minute," he said.

"Does Judy have to sing Hawaiian songs? She knows I want snow."

"Why don't you sing your own carols, Stink? Like . . . *Hark! The herald angels sing!*" Dad belted out.

"Who's this Harold guy everybody's always singing about, anyway?"

"Never mind," said Dad, shaking his head. Stink put on his snowflake costume and sang, *"Let it snow! Let it snow! Let it snow!"*

Just then the doorbell rang. "Pizza!" yelled Stink.

The Moodys sat down to dinner. Judy was the first to grab the pizza table, for her collection. Stink ate all the pineapples off his pizza.

"What a great holiday show you kids had this year," said Dad.

"And I didn't have to be a mouse, for once," said Stink.

"Mrs. D. sure was surprised," Mom said.

"Yeah, she kept saying 'mouse,' and Stink didn't come out."

"My snowflake got stuck in the door to the stage!" said Stink.

Ding, dong.

"Could that be the pizza man *again?*" Dad asked.

"I'll get it!" called Stink. He raced out of the kitchen and opened the front door. Stink could not believe his eyes. It was Jack Frost, live and in person!

"One more package for the Moodys got left behind in my truck," Jack said. "Thought it might be important."

"Wow!" said Stink, taking the package. "I never knew the mailman came at night!"

Jack Frost laughed. "At this time of year, we work long hours."

"Thanks!" said Stink. "So you think it might snow tonight?"

"Never say never," said Jack. "Might be

making snow angels and having snowball fights yet. Well, gotta go. I still have a lot of work to do!"

"Goodbye, Jack Frost! Have a Holly Jolly Day! I mean a Holly Joliday! I mean a Jolly Holiday!

"Did you hear that?" Stink asked his family, coming back into the kitchen.

"We heard you wishing somebody a holly *joliday.*" Judy cracked up. "Who *was* it?"

"Jack Frost."

"Not again," said Judy, rolling her eyes.

"Who's Jack Frost?" Mom and Dad asked at the same time.

"You guys don't know who Jack Frost is?" Stink asked.

58

"He's the new mailman," said Judy.

"And he brings snow," Stink added. "And tonight he brought us a package. Can we open it? Can-we-can-we-can-we?"

"Hmm. No return address on the box," said Dad. "Must be from Grandma Lou."

"She already sent fruitcake," said Mom.

"Maybe it's a yule log," said Judy.

"What's a yule log?" asked Stink.

"*Yule* never know!" Judy cracked up. "Just open it, Stink!"

Stink ripped the tape off the box. Inside were two squishy packages—one marked for Judy, and one for Stink. They tore off the wrapping paper.

"Mittens!" said Stink. A green pair for Stink and a red pair for Judy.

"Fa la la la la," said Judy. "I'd rather have fruitcake."

"That's weird," said Stink. "There's still nothing that says who they're from. Just a note that says, 'You'll need these when the snow flies.'"

"Ooh—it's a mystery," said Judy.

"Maybe they're from Jack Frost!" Stink said.

"So now Jack Frost knows how to knit, too?" Judy snorted. "Stink, why would the mailman give us a present?"

"He's not *just* the mailman," said Stink.

• ● •

After pizza, Judy and Stink went into the playroom. Stink stared out the window. Judy decked the halls with Christmas-in-

Hawaii stuff—she decorated the blow-up palm tree from the holiday show with origami surfboards, sailboats, and sea horses. She hung a string of pink flamingo lights. Even Mouse got to wear a grass skirt and fake flower *lei*.

Stink pointed to the black sky. "I think I see some clouds!"

"I think you're seeing stars, Kimo," said Judy.

"I wish every one of those stars was a snowflake," said Stink. He sighed. "I hope it snows by midnight. Jack Frost said—"

"Stink," Judy said, craning her neck to look up at the sky, "give it up. No way is it going to snow by midnight."

"Wanna bet?" asked Stink.

"Sure," said Judy. "But if I win, *you* have to eat fruitcake."

"Okay, but if I win, you have to help me build a snowman."

"Deal," said Judy.

"Hey, wait just a minute!" said Stink. "How will you know if it snows by mid-night? You'll be in bed, sound asleep by then."

"No way," said Judy. "I'm waiting up."

"Cool yule!" said Stink. "Me, too!"

8:12 p.m.

"No way am I drinking this!" Stink sniffed the yucky-smelling stuff in his Santa mug.

"It's coffee," said Judy. "That's how you stay awake."

"Coffee! Bluck! I'd rather drink a cup of mud."

"Just try it," Judy told her brother.

"Dad, are we allowed?" asked Stink.

"Go ahead. Try it," said Dad. "It's a special occasion."

"C'mon, Kimo," said Judy. "You go first."

Stink stared into the dark murky liquid. He took a sip. *Bluhhh!* He spit it into the sink. "It tastes like tree bark," said Stink. Dad grinned.

"Tree bark?" said Judy. "There must be other ways to stay awake besides drinking tree bark."

8:43 p.m.

Judy and Stink played all the holiday CDs they could find. Mom and Dad sang along to "Frosty the Snowman," "Jingle Bell Rock," and "Winter Wonderland." Stink and Judy sang the Grinch theme song at the top of their lungs:

> *"Your heart is full of unwashed socks;*
> *Your soul is full of gunk, Mr. Grinch!*

The three words that best describe you
Are as follows, and I quote:
STINK . . . STANK . . . STUNK!"

9:15 p.m.

They took turns reading aloud all the books in the house about snow. *Owl Moon* and *The Snowy Day* and *Snowflake Bentley*. Dad even recited the poem "Stopping by Woods on a Snowy Evening."

"All these snowy books are making me sleepy," said Stink.

"All these snowy books are making me cold," said Judy. "Brrrrr!"

9:23 p.m.

Mom and Dad wrapped more presents.

Judy and Stink played fifty-two-card pickup about fifty-three times. "No fair. How come you always get to throw them, and I always have to pick up all the cards?" asked Stink.

9:36 p.m.

"I have a game for us, Stink. I'll ask you a question, and you say, 'Freak of nature.' Ready?"

"Ready, Freddy."

"What's another name for a blizzard in Virginia?"

"Freak of nature."

"What's your favorite subject in school?"

"Freak of nature."

"What do you call somebody who only wants snow for Christmas?"

"Freak of nature. Hey, wait, that's me!"

"Exactly," said Judy.

9:44 p.m.

"Still no snow," said Stink, reporting from his lookout by the window. He pointed to the thermometer outside. "Hey, good news. It's thirty-eight degrees. The temperature's dropping. It was thirty-*nine* a few minutes ago."

"Well, my temperature's going up every time you check that thing!"

9:52 p.m.

"Kids!" said Dad, poking his head into

the playroom. "It's way past your bedtime!"

Mom had ribbon around her neck and a tag stuck to her sweater. "It's past mine, too," she said, yawning.

"But it's Christmas Eve!" said Stink.

"We're trying to stay up till midnight," said Judy. "To see if it snows. Can't we just sleep down here in our sleeping bags tonight?"

Mom and Dad gave each other a look. "Okay," said Dad. "Mom and I are off to bed. No pillow fights."

"And no more hula dancing. Time to start tucking in," said Mom.

"Bah, humbug," said Judy.

She put on her monkey PJs. Stink

climbed inside his snowflake sleeping bag. Mom and Dad kissed them good night and turned out the lights. Stink couldn't help closing his eyes.

"Stink, don't punk out on me now," Judy said, plugging the flamingo lights back in. The palm tree twinkled with all the colors of a sunset in Hawaii.

"I'm just resting my eyes," said Stink, yawning.

10:12 p.m.

Judy went to brush her teeth. By the time she came back, Stink was fast asleep. Even Mouse was curled up on a cozy Santa hat. "Hey, Snoozer," Judy called, but Stink did not wake up. She tried making goofy faces and noises. She tried lifting up his eyelids. She tried tickling him awake with the fuzzy tip of the Santa hat.

Finally, she gave up. Stink was going to be so bummed out that he fell asleep. But he was going to be double disappointed when he woke up and there was no snow.

10:27 p.m.

Judy hummed all Twelve Days of Christmas . . . inside her head.

10:28 p.m.

Judy counted reindeer . . . inside her head.

10:37 p.m.

Suddenly, in the not-so-silent night, Judy heard something . . . tapping on the roof. *Reindeer?* She heard something else . . . tapping at the window. *Jack Frost?* She looked out, when what to her wondering eyes did appear, but . . .

Rain!

There was only one thing worse than *not* getting snow for Christmas. Getting *rain.* Judy looked over at the sleeping Stink. He was going to be double triple quadruple bummed-out disappointed.

What happened then? Well, in Moodyville they say that Judy Moody's heart grew three sizes that day.

Judy ran to get scissors. Paper. Glitter. Glue. *Snip, snip, snip.* While Stink was asleep all snug on the couch, Judy made millions of paper snowflakes and stuck them all over the walls, windows, and doors.

She sprinkled the teeny-tiny scraps along the windowsill and all across the floor. She even sprinkled Stink while he was sleeping. In the moonlight, the confetti looked like new-fallen snow.

Perfect! *Brain*storms were better than *rain*storms any old day. Now Stink could have a ho-ho, not ho-hum, Christmas. Judy could not wait to see Stink's face when he woke up to snow everywhere, even if it was fake. It would be a million times better than watching him eat fruitcake any day.

Judy felt like Old Man Winter. She felt like Santa at the North Pole. She felt like Snow Freak Bentley.

She, Judy Moody, felt like the genuine-and-for-real Jack not-the-mailman Frost.

11:57 p.m.

Just before the big hand and the little hand hit twelve, the rain stopped tap, tap, tapping. Judy snuggled down into her cozy sleeping bag. At last, she was ready for some long winter's nap, nap, napping.

When Stink woke up bright and early Christmas morning, he thought he was dreaming.

"Judy! Wake up! Wake up! Snow! It really is a white Christmas!"

Judy rolled over. "I know, Stink. It's just pretend snow. I didn't want you to have a very muddy Christmas. Or a very moody one."

"No, Jack Frost was here. For real and absolute positive. No lie."

"Um-hmmm. He brought us mittens,"

said Judy, hunkering down into her sleeping bag. "It's cold!"

"C'mon, Bed Head." Stink tugged at her sleeping bag. "Just get up and look out the window."

Still wrapped in her sleeping bag, Judy stood up and kangaroo-hopped over to the window. Stink had rubbed a small circle in the frost on the windowpane. Judy and Stink smushed their noses to the glass and peered out. Mouse dashed over to the window, too, jingling all the way.

Snow. Real-live, not-fake snow. On houses, trees, rocks, hills, and leaves. Everywhere they looked, a blanket of white. A marvelous marshmallow world. A whipped-cream winter wonderland.

The earth was covered in clean, bright, stellar-dendrite snow. Heaven and nature seemed to sparkle and sing. Joy to the world!

"Snow," Stink breathed. Now he could see why, in Alaska, they had a dozen different words for snow. One word just wasn't good enough.

"A genuine-and-for-real freak of nature!" said Judy.

"It's like being inside a snow globe—from Vermont!" said Stink. "I wished. I hoped. I dreamed of a white Christmas, and my wish came true. Just like Jack Frost said."

"The world is your snowball, Stink!" said Judy.

• ● •

Then Judy and Stink took one look at each other. Away to the closet they flew like a flash. They pulled on their boots and they pulled on their hats. They pulled on their coats and their scarves and their brand-new, hand-knit mystery mittens.

They held their breath as they opened the front door.

Judy and Stink stepped outside into the snowy-blowy, swirly-twirly winter wonderland.

"Rare!" said Judy.

"Cool yule!" said Stink. "This is the best holly joliday ever!"

*Judy Moody and Stink go on a hilarious
swashbuckling adventure in . . .*

Judy Moody & Stink
THE MAD,
MAD, MAD, MAD
TREASURE HUNT

Arrr, matey, you'll be able to find out more online at
www.judymoody.com and **www.stinkmoody.com.**